Dedicated to you with retro horror love.

May you always find a reason to smile.

Dead End Drive – In
A Retro Horrors: The Lost Decade Book
Meant to be read in no particular order.
By: B. Humphrey

Contents

Chapter 1: The Storm Rolls In
October 14th, 1986 – Rustwood Drive-In Theater

The night crackled with the kind of magic that only October could conjure. A brisk autumn wind carried the scent of caramel apples, wet leaves, and wood smoke across the Rustwood Drive-In's lot, winding through rows of parked cars. A thousand little details wove together—jack-o'-lantern air fresheners dangling from rearview mirrors, the faint clink of beer bottles in paper bags, and the hum of idling engines mixing with the soundtrack of *Night of the Living Dead*. The sky was an oil-slick black, heavy with clouds that swallowed the moon.

Elliot "El" Monroe sat on the tailgate of Tyler's pickup truck, the thin wool of his letterman jacket doing little to fight the autumn chill. The scratchy radio perched on the truck's cab hissed as it fought for a signal, offering garbled snippets of 80s pop hits. A mix of *Simple Minds* and *Dire Straits* flickered in and out, lost in the night like a forgotten broadcast from some otherworldly station. El could smell popcorn wafting from the concession stand, buttery and warm, cutting through the damp air.

Cassie Whitmore—El's best friend, and the reason he was slowly freezing his ass off on a Wednesday night—grinned at him from her spot on the truck bed. The pink streak in her jet-black hair gleamed under the drive-in's neon lights. She wore a patched-up leather jacket over a threadbare *Misfits* tee, her scuffed combat boots dangling off the side of the truck like she didn't have a care in the world.

"I'm telling you, Romero's zombies are the best," Cassie declared, her voice sharp with conviction. "No running, no crazy mutations, just slow, creepy death. They get in your head. Like existential dread in shambling corpse form."

El shook his head, tossing a popcorn kernel into his mouth. "Nah. You need a slasher villain. Someone iconic—Freddy, Jason, Michael. They've got *presence*. A good villain needs style."

"Freddy's a fashion disaster." Cassie scoffed. "Sweater and a fedora? Really?" Ty Granger leaned over the cab, smirking as he zipped up his *Top Gun* jacket. "How do you even know what existential dread is, Cass?" Cassie shot him a playful glare. "Because I've read books, Ty. Not that you'd know anything about that."

El laughed as Ty gave a mock-wounded expression, but before the banter could continue, Becca Turner climbed into the truck bed with a clatter of boots. She was a whirlwind of red curls, flannel layers, and Polaroid cameras slung around her neck. The lenses clinked together as she sat cross-legged, popping open a can of soda.

"Got the last of the Mountain Dew," Becca said, holding it up like a prize. "There's a line at the concession stand already. Everyone's here for pizza night." Ty groaned. "Of course they are. Now we're stuck with popcorn." Becca leaned in, flashing a mischievous grin. "Unless someone distracts the guy at the counter..."

"I'm not getting kicked out," El said, though the idea tempted him. Before anyone could follow up with another bad idea, the sky rumbled with a distant growl of thunder. A low hush fell over the crowd, and people craned their necks toward the sky.

"That's new," El muttered. "It wasn't supposed to rain tonight." The first fat drops splattered against the truck's hood, and the smell of damp asphalt filled the air. Someone cursed loudly from across the lot, and a few people scrambled to roll up their windows. The storm blew in fast, the wind snapping through the trees and rattling the tin awning over the concession stand.

The radio sputtered again, the signal falling apart into white noise and static. El tapped it, frowning. "It's not even raining that hard."

But the weather wasn't the only thing that felt off. As the wind picked up, the picture on the drive-in screen flickered, the black-and-white zombies of *Night of the Living Dead* stuttering in and out. One moment, Barbara was fleeing the cemetery zombie, and the next, the screen glitched—her image fracturing into shards of light.

El shivered, goosebumps crawling up his arms. A gust of cold air swept through the truck bed, and suddenly everything felt *wrong*. Cassie nudged him with her elbow. "That was weird, right?"

"Yeah," El whispered, his eyes locked on the screen. "Really weird." The thunder rumbled again, closer this time, and with it came a flash of lightning that struck somewhere near the projection booth. The neon sign above the lot buzzed and flickered, casting the words *Rustwood Drive-In* in jagged, erratic flashes.

And that's when El noticed the first zombie. It stood near the back of the lot, just outside the range of the headlights. At first, El thought it was some weirdo in costume—someone trying too hard to get into the spirit of the movie. The figure shuffled forward, its head tilted at an unnatural angle. Its skin was an ashen gray, and one arm hung limp at its side.

Cassie squinted. "Is... is that a costume?" El's stomach twisted. He knew horror movies, he'd seen every zombie flick worth watching, and there was something disturbingly *real* about the way this one moved.

Before he could answer, the figure lunged at a group of teenagers leaning against a Ford Pinto. There was a scream - sharp and shrill - and chaos erupted. The teens scattered, knocking over lawn chairs and spilling sodas as the zombie tackled one of them to the ground.

"What the hell?" Ty shouted, leaping off the truck bed. "Stay here," El said quickly, grabbing Cassie's arm. "Something's not right." Becca snapped a Polaroid picture, the flash illuminating the scene for an instant. "That... that's not normal."

The crowd broke into confusion, some people laughing nervously, others backing away from the apparent attack. And then the zombie bit the boy on the ground. Blood sprayed across the asphalt, hot and dark in the cold night air.

El's heart raced. "We need to get out of here." But before they could move, the projector sputtered and jumped again. The image on the screen shifted, Barbara's terrified face morphing into something else entirely. The drive-in screen crackled with static, and a new movie started to bleed through: *Halloween.*

The crowd gasped as Michael Myers appeared, knife gleaming in the moonlight. And then... *he stepped off the screen.*

The shape of Michael Myers moved with deliberate, silent menace, his expressionless mask gleaming in the neon haze. He walked between the cars, his knife catching the light with each smooth step. The laughter died abruptly, replaced by panicked shouts as people stumbled over one another to get away. Cassie grabbed El's sleeve. "Tell me this is some kind of weird publicity stunt."

"It's not," El whispered. More figures emerged from the screen, crossing the threshold between reel and reality. A slasher in a hockey mask. A gremlin with wicked, glowing eyes. Even the faintest strains of eerie music seemed to follow them—like each monster brought their own soundtracks.

Ty jumped into the cab of the truck, yanking the door open. "We gotta go. Now." Becca's hands shook as she rewound the Polaroid camera, the snap-click noise too loud against the sudden quiet. "How... how is this happening?"

El didn't have an answer. All he knew was that they needed to get the hell out of there. "Come on!" he shouted, dragging Cassie toward the truck's passenger side.

The wind howled through the drive-in, carrying with it the scent of ozone and decayed leaves. Cars screeched to life, engines revving as people tried to escape. But the parking lot was a maze of panic, and the monsters seemed to move faster than the fleeing crowd.

El clambered into the truck just as Michael Myers reached for the handle of a nearby car. His mask gleamed in the headlights, blank and emotionless.

"We're not gonna make it," Cassie muttered, her breath visible in the cold air. Ty slammed the truck into gear, tires squealing against the pavement. "We'll make it," he said, though the fear in his voice was unmistakable.

They tore through the lot, narrowly avoiding a gremlin that darted under the wheels. El looked back toward the screen just in time to see the projector flicker again—more shapes shifting, more horrors bleeding into the real world.

"This is bad," El whispered. "Really, really bad."

The storm surged overhead, and the last thing El saw before the truck barreled through the exit was the flickering sign above the drive-in, sputtering out in a final, jagged flash:

Rustwood Drive-In—Dead End.

And so it begins, the first night of their descent into a world where horror no longer obeys the rules of fiction. The storm has unleashed something ancient, and there's no escaping it. Not until the last reel ends. Or until they do.

Chapter 2: The First Transformation

October 14th, 1986 – Rustwood Drive-In

The truck's tires shrieked as they skidded around the curve onto the dirt road leading out of the drive-in. El's heart hammered against his ribs, every breath sharp with adrenaline. The truck bed rattled under the weight of supplies, half-empty popcorn bags, cans of soda rolling loose, and the muffled shouts of other moviegoers trapped in the drive-in echoed behind them.

Cassie leaned out of the passenger window, her jacket flapping wildly in the wind. "We can't leave them!" she shouted over the roar of the engine. Ty clenched his jaw, gripping the wheel. "We'll get help! What do you want me to do? Fight Michael Myers with a box of Milk Duds?"

In the rearview mirror, El saw the monsters spreading out across the lot, stalking between cars and dragging people into the shadows. The giant screen behind them continued to flicker and jump, images overlapping—one moment *Night of the Living Dead*, the next *Gremlins* and *Friday the 13th*.

The headlights bounced as they hit a pothole, and Ty cursed under his breath, his knuckles white on the steering wheel. El turned back toward Becca, who was sitting in the truck bed, her arms clutching her Polaroid camera like it was a life preserver.

"Becca!" El called out. "You okay?" Becca gave him a shaky thumbs-up but said nothing, her face pale under the dim lights of the dashboard. El knew she was trying to piece together what they'd just seen—trying to make sense of it all. But no amount of logic was going to explain how fictional monsters had come to life.

Cassie climbed back into the truck, slamming the door shut. "We need to figure out what's going on. This isn't some weird prank, El. People are... changing." The word hung in the air, heavy with implication. El glanced at her, the weight of the realization sinking in. It wasn't just monsters coming off the screen. People—regular people—were starting to *become* them.

Ty screeched the truck to a halt in the parking lot of the gas station just outside the drive-in. The neon sign above the building buzzed with that familiar electrical hum, casting flickering pink light over the cracked pavement.

They sat in silence for a moment, the engine ticking as it cooled. El rubbed his hands over his face, trying to think. "What the hell just happened?"

Cassie ran a hand through her hair, chewing on her lip. "I don't know... but we can't go back in there without a plan."

Becca climbed out of the truck bed and leaned against the side of the vehicle, her breath visible in the cold air. "My dad was trying to shut the projector off." Her voice was small, barely audible. "He said it was... dangerous. I thought he was just being dramatic."

El looked at her, a knot tightening in his chest. "You think the projector caused this?" Becca nodded slowly. "Yeah. It has to be. But it's not just the movies coming to life. People are... changing. It's like the film's rewriting them."

Cassie crossed her arms, pacing. "So, what? We just turn off the projector and everything goes back to normal?" Becca shook her head. "It's not that simple. My dad always said there was something... cursed about it. Like it was tied to the film reels somehow. If we shut it off wrong, it could make things worse."

Ty groaned, resting his forehead against the steering wheel. "How could it get worse?" El leaned against the truck, his mind racing. "If people are turning into the monsters they watched... it's only a matter of time before we lose everyone in that drive-in."

Cassie stopped pacing and looked at him. "What if we're next?" A heavy silence fell over them. The idea sat in the back of El's mind like a cold, sharp weight—what if, at some point, they stopped being themselves? What if the horror got inside them, too?

The gas station's door jingled open, and an old man wearing a grease-stained cap shuffled out, lighting a cigarette. He squinted at the group, his expression somewhere between concern and mild amusement.

"You kids okay?" he asked, blowing smoke into the autumn air. El exchanged a look with Cassie, unsure how to respond. What could they even say? *We're running from Michael Myers?* The guy would think they were nuts. "Yeah," El muttered. "Just passing through." The man shrugged, taking a drag from his cigarette. "Storm like this? Ain't nobody 'just passing through.'"

As the man retreated back inside, Ty kicked at the gravel beneath his feet. "So, what now? We go back and fight off a bunch of movie monsters? Because that's not exactly in my skillset." Cassie gave him a playful shove. "What's the matter, Maverick? Afraid of a little slasher action?" Ty rolled his eyes. "I signed up for 'Top Gun,' not 'Halloween.'"

El tried not to laugh, but the tension in the air made it impossible to relax. Every instinct in his body told him they had to go back—but they couldn't go in blind. "We need to get to the projection booth," he said finally. "If we can figure out what's wrong with the projector, maybe we can stop this before it spreads."

Cassie cracked her knuckles. "All right. What's the plan, then?" El looked at each of them, weighing their options. "We sneak back in, get to the booth, and find Becca's dad. He might know how to shut everything down." Ty raised an eyebrow. "And if we run into, you know... the boogeyman?" El tried to muster a grin. "Then we follow the rules."

Cassie grinned back. "Rule number one: Never split up." - "Rule number two," El added, "don't be the idiot who investigates strange noises." Ty shook his head in disbelief. "We are so screwed."

Becca climbed back into the truck bed, slinging her Polaroid camera over her shoulder. "If we're going back in there," she said, "we're going to need more than just movie trivia to get through this." El climbed into the cab beside Ty. "We'll make it work. We have to."

As Ty started the engine, the storm thickened overhead, thunder rumbling like the soundtrack to a nightmare. The wind howled through the pines, carrying with it the eerie scent of popcorn, wet leaves, and something else—something cold and unnatural.

They were going back into the drive-in.

And this time, the horror wouldn't wait.

Chapter 3: Escape from Michael Myers

October 14th, 1986 – Rustwood Drive-In

The drive-in loomed through the storm, neon lights flickering weakly under the weight of the rain-soaked sky. Rows of parked cars sat like silent witnesses to the unfolding nightmare. El's heart pounded in his chest as Ty's truck rolled back through the entrance, the tires crunching over the gravel.

The air smelled like damp asphalt, popcorn, and gasoline. But underneath it all, there was a creeping scent—something metallic and rotting, like the stink of old film reels left to fester.

The screen at the center of the lot flickered madly, switching from scenes of *Night of the Living Dead* to the chilling score of *Halloween*. As the eerie piano notes filled the air, El's stomach turned cold. They weren't alone. Cassie leaned forward, squinting through the windshield. "There he is."

The towering figure of Michael Myers emerged from the shadows, his kitchen knife glinting beneath the neon sign of the concession stand. He moved with unnerving calm, the heavy steps of a predator who knew his prey had nowhere to run. "Holy shit," Ty muttered, gripping the steering wheel tighter.

Becca gasped from the truck bed, snapping a Polaroid just as Myers turned his head, the pale mask catching the light. El felt his pulse quicken. Seeing Michael Myers up close, not on a screen but here in real life, was like watching a childhood nightmare break free of its leash. "What's the plan?" Cassie whispered, her voice taut.

"We get to the booth," El said, not sure if he was convincing her or himself. "If we shut down the projector, this whole thing ends." Michael took another step forward, head tilting as if he could sense them. "Drive, Ty!" El shouted.

Ty floored the gas, and the truck roared to life, wheels kicking up gravel as they tore toward the concession stand. Michael's silhouette grew smaller in the rearview mirror, but El knew they hadn't seen the last of him.

The concession stand stood at the heart of the lot, lit by flickering neon signs advertising popcorn, soda, and pizza. The glass windows rattled in the wind, and the candy machines inside buzzed faintly. El and Cassie leapt from the truck, hitting the ground running. "Come on!" El shouted, leading the way toward the projection booth.

The storm whipped around them, rain slashing sideways through the night. As they sprinted across the parking lot, El noticed strange movements at the edge of his vision—zombies shambling between the cars, gremlin-like creatures scurrying in the shadows.

Becca slid down from the truck bed, clutching her Polaroid camera like a weapon. She snapped a photo of one of the zombies—a blurry image of dead eyes and slack jaws. "This is insane," she whispered, more to herself than anyone else.

Cassie grabbed her arm, pulling her along. "Come on, Becca. We need to move." The projection booth loomed ahead, a squat, graffiti-covered building at the far end of the lot. A dull yellow bulb buzzed above the door, casting just enough light to show the scratched metal handle.

El reached the door first and yanked it open. "Inside, now!" Cassie and Becca rushed in behind him, and Ty slammed the door shut, the heavy clang reverberating through the small space. They stood there for a moment, catching their breath.

The projection booth smelled like burnt popcorn and stale cigarettes, with a faint undercurrent of mildew. An old reel-to-reel projector sat in the center of the room, its lens cracked and coated in dust. Film canisters were scattered across the floor, their labels faded and unreadable.

"Where's your dad?" El asked Becca, his eyes scanning the room. Becca shook her head, her voice shaky. "I don't know. He was supposed to be here." Ty leaned against the wall, wiping rain from his brow. "Great. So now what?"

Cassie walked over to the projector, running her fingers along the side. "This thing's ancient. Are we sure this is what's causing all of this?" Becca knelt by a stack of film canisters, flipping through them. "These reels... they're not supposed to be here. My dad said this booth hadn't been used in years. Something must've reactivated it."

El crouched beside her, picking up one of the film reels. The metal was cold to the touch, and strange symbols were scratched into the surface—arcane markings that made his skin crawl. "This doesn't feel right," he muttered. "Yeah, no kidding," Cassie said, peering through the window toward the lot. "And we've got company."

El followed her gaze and felt his stomach drop. Michael Myers was back, his silhouette framed by the neon lights of the lot. He stood perfectly still, the knife in his hand gleaming like a promise.

"We need to shut this thing down," El said, his voice low. Becca fiddled with the projector's controls, her hands trembling. "I don't know how... If we stop it wrong, it could—"

A deafening *bang* cut her off, the door to the booth shaking on its hinges. El jumped back, his heart in his throat. Michael Myers was outside, testing the door. "He's coming," Ty whispered, his voice tight with fear. Cassie grabbed a heavy film reel from the floor. "We fight him off. Just like in the movies."

"That's not how it works," El said, panic rising in his chest. "This isn't a movie. If he gets in here, we're dead." Another bang echoed through the booth, the door buckling under the weight of Michael's relentless assault. "We don't have time!" Becca shouted, her fingers flying over the projector's controls. "If I can just—"

The projector flickered, and for a brief moment, the screen outside switched to another movie: *Friday the 13th*. A new shape emerged from the screen, a hulking figure with a hockey mask and a machete.

"Oh, come on!" Ty groaned. "Not Jason too!" The door burst open, and Michael Myers stepped inside, his knife gleaming. Cassie threw the film reel at him, but it bounced off his shoulder with a dull thud. He didn't even flinch.

"RUN!" El shouted. The group scattered, dodging past the slasher as he swung his knife in a slow, deliberate arc. Becca yanked a film reel from the projector, and the screen outside flickered again, jumping between movies. The storm outside raged harder, wind howling through the broken door.

They needed to act fast, or this nightmare was going to get a lot worse. El grabbed Becca's arm, pulling her toward the exit. "We need to shut this thing down—now!" Becca fumbled with the reel in her hands. "I think... I think this one might be the key!" Cassie darted past Michael, narrowly avoiding his knife. "Just do it, Becca!"

Becca slammed the reel into place, her fingers trembling as she cranked the projector. The machine whirred to life, and the images on the screen began to stabilize. The sound of thunder rumbled through the night, and the figures outside flickered, their forms wavering like static on a broken TV. "It's working!" El shouted.

But Michael Myers didn't waver. He kept coming, his mask blank and unrelenting. Cassie grabbed a chair and swung it at him, buying them precious seconds. "How do we stop him?" Becca twisted the projector's knobs, her face pale with concentration. "I just need a little more time—"

But they were out of time. Michael raised his knife, and El knew they had one shot left. He grabbed the nearest film canister and hurled it at the projector, smashing it to pieces.

The screen outside flickered one last time—and then everything went dark. The monsters vanished. The storm eased. And the world outside the booth was quiet once more. But El knew, deep down, that the nightmare wasn't over. Not yet.

"Let's get out of here," he whispered. And together, they slipped into the night, knowing full well that the horror was far from finished.

Chapter 4: The Thing in the Playground

October 14th, 1986 – Rustwood Drive-In

The air outside was different, heavy with a strange stillness that made El's skin prickle. The flickering movie screen behind them had gone dark, but the night wasn't quiet—it was that kind of unnatural silence that settles before something terrible happens.

The group moved quickly through the lot, weaving between abandoned cars. Steam rose from hoods still hot from running engines, and rainwater pooled in cracks along the pavement. A dull, coppery scent lingered in the air—blood, fresh and mingling with the smell of wet asphalt. El glanced toward the screen, half-expecting it to spring back to life, but all that remained was a dull hum in the projector booth behind them.

"We can't keep running," Becca whispered, gripping her Polaroid like a lifeline. Her curls clung to her rain-damp face, and her breath puffed out in quick clouds. "We need to regroup."

"Where?" Ty hissed. "Everything's crawling with monsters!" Cassie, ever the brave one, scanned the lot with sharp eyes. Her boots splashed in a puddle as she pointed toward the playground on the far side of the drive-in. A warped swing set and rusty monkey bars gleamed under the hazy glow of a malfunctioning streetlight. "There," she said. "We can hole up in the fort until we figure this out."

"The fort?" Ty asked, looking like she'd just suggested they crawl into a coffin. "Unless you want to go back and fight Michael Myers." Cassie shot him a grin. "Didn't think so."

El took the lead, heart pounding, as they sprinted toward the playground. Shadows twisted in the corners of his vision—zombies shifting between cars, something small and snarling darting beneath a Buick, chewing on what appeared to be the half-eaten remains of somebody. The storm still rumbled overhead, and the wind rattled the metal chains of the swings, setting them into slow, creaking motion.

They reached the playground just as something scuttled across the parking lot behind them—a flicker of movement too fast to track. El whipped his head around, catching sight of a glimmering pair of eyes in the shadows.

"Gremlins," he whispered, tightening his grip on his jacket. "Of course there are gremlins." Cassie climbed up into the playground fort, the wooden boards creaking under her weight. "Well, at least it's not *The Thing*." As if summoned by her words, a low growl reverberated from somewhere inside the playground. El froze. "Why would you say that?"

The growl came again, this time closer—a wet, throaty sound that made El's skin crawl. The air turned colder, and a foul stench hit him, like meat left to rot in the sun. "Guys?" Becca whispered, her voice tight. "Something's here."

They huddled inside the small wooden fort, the walls closing in around them. Rain dripped through cracks in the roof, and the air inside smelled like mold and old wood. Cassie crouched by one of the small windows, peeking out toward the lot.

"Anything out there?" El whispered, his voice low. Cassie shook her head. "No Myers, no zombies... but something's *here*."

A slithering sound echoed from beneath the playground structure—something wet dragging itself across the dirt. El's pulse quickened. He knew that sound. He'd heard it in *The Thing*, during the autopsy scene.

"Don't move," El whispered. "Don't say a word."

The Thing moved closer, its body shifting and reshaping as it crawled into the fort's shadow. Rainwater dripped off its grotesque form, each droplet hitting the ground with an audible plink. El knew the rules—The Thing could look like anyone, *become* anyone. Trust was no longer an option.

Cassie met his gaze, her eyes wide with understanding. If any one of them had been infected by The Thing, it could mean the end of them all. "What do we do?" Ty whispered, his breath fogging the air. El swallowed hard. "We test each other." Becca gasped, clutching her Polaroid camera tight. "How do we test for... for *that*?"

El thought fast. "We use the Polaroid. The flash might mess with it—force it to reveal itself." Cassie nodded. "Makes sense. In the movie, it couldn't mimic human behavior perfectly. Maybe it can't handle the light."

"Or maybe it can," Ty muttered grimly. Becca took a shaky breath, raising her Polaroid. "Okay... who's first?" The Thing shifted below them, the grotesque slithering sound growing louder. El could feel the weight of its presence pressing against the wooden walls, like it was testing their defenses, waiting for a weakness.

"Just do it," El said, holding still. "Take the picture." The camera clicked. The flash ignited, blinding them for a split second. Becca yanked the photo free and shook it nervously. "Please be normal... please be normal..." The image developed slowly, the familiar hiss of chemicals filling the silence. A blurry shape emerged, El, blinking in the harsh light, looking very much like himself.

Cassie exhaled sharply. "He's good." They went one by one each picture revealing their normal faces, no twisted mutations, no grotesque imitations. For a moment, it seemed like they were safe.

Until they heard the laugh. The sound was high-pitched and jagged, like nails dragged across a chalkboard. It came from below, rising through the slats of the playground floor. El's heart stopped as a small, wrinkled hand appeared on the edge of the fort—a gremlin, its wicked grin gleaming in the dim light. "Gremlins *and* The Thing?" Ty groaned. "We are *so* dead."

Cassie grabbed a loose wooden board and swung it at the creature, knocking it back. "Not yet, we're not." The Thing shifted again, merging with the shadows, its grotesque body reshaping as it pursued them. Gremlins scampered out from the dark corners of the playground, their cackles filling the air. "Go!" El shouted, shoving Cassie toward the exit. "Get to the lot!"

They scrambled out of the fort, slipping on the rain-slick wood as they ran for the parking lot. Gremlins darted around their feet, clawing and biting, but Cassie kicked them aside with her boots.

El glanced back just in time to see the twisted form of The Thing slithering into the light, its grotesque body writhing with impossible shapes. His stomach lurched—it was worse than anything the movie had shown.

They hit the pavement running, the gremlins snapping at their heels. The storm roared overhead, and the flickering neon lights cast eerie shadows across the lot. "Where do we go?" Ty shouted, panic in his voice. El's mind raced. They needed a plan—fast. "Concession stand! We make a stand there!"

Cassie grinned through the rain, her adrenaline pumping. "Hell yeah. Let's give these little bastards a fight." Together, they sprinted toward the glowing lights of the concession stand, the storm raging around them and the monsters closing in.

The nightmare wasn't over—not even close. And the night had only just begun.

Chapter 5: Becca's Discovery
October 14th, 1986 – Rustwood Drive-In,
Concession Stand

The group huddled inside the dim, flickering light of the concession stand. Rain pattered against the warped metal roof, and the windows rattled in their frames with each gust of wind. The air smelled of burnt popcorn and stale soda syrup, mixing with the metallic scent of the storm outside. Every shadow felt alive, shifting as though the monsters still lurked, just waiting to strike.

Cassie leaned back against a counter, wiping her face with the sleeve of her leather jacket. "We need to figure this out. Fast. The longer we wait, the more people out there get... changed."

"Changed? Try *murdered*," Ty muttered, rubbing the back of his neck nervously. "We need to blow up that projector or something." Becca, still shaking from their mad dash to the stand, dropped her backpack to the sticky floor and unzipped it with trembling hands. "We can't just destroy it. If we do this wrong... it could make everything worse." Cassie shot her a sharp look. "Define 'worse.' Worse than *zombies* and *Michael freakin' Myers*?"

Becca dug through the clutter inside her backpack, flashlights, batteries, spare film cartridges, until she pulled out a worn, leather-bound notebook. Its pages were yellowed and soft with age, and strange symbols were scrawled across the cracked cover. She turned it over in her hands like it weighed a thousand pounds. "This was my dad's," she whispered, her voice tight. "He tried to warn me... He said the reel wasn't just a movie. It's a prison."

El knelt beside her, the rain-soaked hem of his jacket leaving a puddle on the floor. He tilted his head, peering at the strange journal. "A prison? For what?"

Becca took a shaky breath and opened the notebook. The brittle pages made a dry, rasping sound, and her fingers hesitated on the edges, like she was afraid of what they might reveal. "It wasn't just some weird film experiment," she said quietly. "The reel and the projector—there's a whole history behind them. A group of producers and directors back in the early days of Hollywood. They wanted to bottle fear. Not just make scary movies—*capture* it. Trap it, like you'd trap an animal."

El felt the air in the room shift as Becca's words sank in. It was one thing to be chased by monsters—it was another to know those monsters weren't the worst thing lurking behind the screen. "And... what did they trap?"

Becca's hands hovered over a page filled with arcane symbols—circles and spirals, intersecting lines, glyphs that didn't belong to any known language. "Something worse," she whispered, flipping through the pages. "Something... alive." A chill ran through El's body, like someone had walked over his grave. "So, every time someone plays the reel..."

"It tries to escape," Becca finished grimly. "It's been trying for years. If the projector plays a cursed reel all the way through without the proper ritual to seal it, the creatures get out—and they don't go back. They bleed into the real world." Cassie let out a slow breath, visibly shaken for the first time all night. "So it's not just a movie marathon. It's a door."

"Exactly," Becca said. "And if the projector breaks—or if we destroy the reel without finishing the ritual—the curse spreads.

It won't stop here. It'll... it'll keep going. Every film, every nightmare, pulled through that door into our world."

Ty leaned his head back against the soda machine, rubbing his temples. "This just keeps getting better and better." El leaned closer to the journal, his brow furrowed. "So what's the plan? How do we close the door?"

Becca flipped to the back of the journal, revealing a set of instructions written in faded ink. Some parts were smeared beyond recognition, but the gist of it was clear: they had to reattach the cursed reel to the projector and complete the binding spell. Only then would the monsters be sucked back inside.

"We have to finish the ritual," Becca said, her voice steady now. "The projector needs the reel to run—once we bind the creatures inside, we can destroy the whole thing. But we have to *complete* the ritual first. If the film stops or the reel breaks, we're screwed."

Cassie groaned. "And here I thought blowing stuff up would solve our problems." El studied the journal's ritual instructions, a knot of anxiety forming in his gut. "This... this sounds complicated. What if we mess it up?"

"We won't," Becca said firmly, though her hands still trembled as she clutched the notebook. "We can't." Ty threw up his hands. "So, just to recap—if we play the reel and screw up the ritual, the monsters stay. If we don't play it at all, the curse spreads anyway. Either way, we're toast."

Cassie shot him a grin, but it didn't reach her eyes. "Welcome to horror movie logic, Maverick." El exhaled slowly, running a hand through his damp hair. "Then we don't screw it up. We follow the instructions. We do the ritual. We end this."

"Easy as that," Ty muttered sarcastically. "Because nothing's gone wrong so far." Becca slammed the notebook shut, her expression determined. "We do it right, or we don't do it at all."

They sat in tense silence for a moment, the storm still howling outside, battering the walls of the concession stand. El leaned back against the counter, processing everything he'd just learned. The projector wasn't just a machine—it was a doorway. A curse. And whatever was trapped inside that reel wasn't just a collection of movie monsters. It was something worse. Cassie cleared her throat, forcing a grin. "Well, no pressure, right?"

El managed a small smile in return, but the weight of what lay ahead pressed down on him like a lead weight. If they failed—if the reel broke or the ritual faltered—this wouldn't end at the drive-in. The monsters would spread beyond the lot, into the streets, into people's homes. The whole town would be a playground for every nightmare ever imagined.

He couldn't let that happen.

Cassie stood and stretched her arms over her head, flashing her usual grin. "So, what are we waiting for? Let's go save the world." Ty groaned but got to his feet. "You're way too excited about this."

Becca slung her backpack over her shoulder, the leather journal tucked safely inside. "We need to get back to the projector before it's too late. We've only got one shot at this." El nodded, his resolve hardening. "One shot."

They exchanged glances, a silent understanding passing between them. They were scared out of their minds, but there was no turning back now. "Okay," El said, straightening his shoulders. "Let's end this."

As they moved toward the door, the wind outside howled and a distant crackle of static buzzed through the drive-in speakers, as if the cursed reel was already stirring to life, waiting for its chance.

With the journal in hand and the knowledge of what they were truly up against, the group stepped out into the storm. Whatever horrors lay ahead, they would face them together. The nightmare wasn't over—not yet. But if they did everything right, it soon would be.

Or so they hoped.

Chapter 6: The Curse Unfolds

October 14th, 1986 – Rustwood Drive-In, Back Lot

The storm howled like a living thing as El, Cassie, Ty, and Becca crept through the back lot, following Becca's flashlight beam as it flickered through the rain-soaked darkness. The projector booth loomed in the distance, its broken window a jagged grin against the night sky. The occasional flicker of lightning lit up the lot, giving El brief glimpses of the nightmare unfolding around them—zombies dragging themselves and helpless victims between cars, gremlins scampering in the puddles, and in the distance, the unmistakable silhouette of Michael Myers.

"We stick to the plan," El whispered, glancing at the others. "Get to the booth, reattach the reel, and finish the ritual. We stop this thing before it spreads."

"And if it doesn't work?" Ty asked, his voice low, but tight with fear. El met his eyes. "It'll work. It has to." They moved quickly and silently through the lot, skirting the edges of the playground and weaving between rows of abandoned cars. Each step felt heavier than the last, the air thick with tension and dread. El's pulse pounded in his ears, but he forced himself to stay focused. They didn't have time to second-guess themselves.

Halfway to the booth, they heard the sound of slow, deliberate footsteps—heavy boots striking the wet pavement. Cassie peeked around the side of a Volkswagen Beetle, her heart-shaped face illuminated by the glow of Becca's flashlight. "You're not gonna like this," she whispered. El crouched beside her, and his stomach dropped.

Jason Voorhees stood in the center of the lot, his hulking figure illuminated by the flickering light of the projector. Rain glistened on his hockey mask, and his machete gleamed like a razor. He stood perfectly still, but there was something about the way he held himself—like a predator waiting for the right moment to strike. Ty cursed under his breath. "We are *so* dead."

"Not yet," El whispered. "Stay low. Move slowly. We can get past him." Cassie rolled her eyes. "Why is it always the slow-moving killers that are the scariest?"

They crept along the side of the lot, every muscle tensed as Jason's masked face turned slowly in their direction. The storm masked the sound of their footsteps, but El could feel Jason's presence—heavy, oppressive, and unrelenting.

Becca's flashlight flickered again, the weak beam skimming across Jason's mask for the briefest moment. El held his breath, praying they wouldn't draw his attention.

Suddenly, a loud *clang* echoed through the lot as something metal toppled over—a trash can kicked by a gremlin scampering toward the playground. Jason's head jerked toward the sound, and he took a step forward, his machete scraping against the pavement. "Go!" El hissed, shoving Cassie toward the booth.

They sprinted through the rain, the beam of Becca's flashlight bouncing wildly as they made a mad dash for the projection booth. Jason moved behind them, slow but deliberate, his heavy footsteps relentless in their pursuit.

El threw open the booth's door, and they tumbled inside, slamming it shut just as Jason reached the threshold. The door rattled as he tested the handle, his machete tapping against the glass window in slow, deliberate knocks.

Becca fumbled with the film reel, yanking it out of her backpack with shaking hands. "We need to get this running," she whispered. "Now." Cassie braced the door with her back, her boots squeaking against the wet floor. "Whatever you're doing, do it fast!" El knelt by the ancient projector, flipping switches and twisting knobs. "How do we know it'll work?"

"We don't," Becca said, slotting the reel into place with a click. "But if we don't try, we're all dead anyway." The projector sputtered to life, the lens flickering as the film reel began to unwind. Strange symbols danced across the frame, glowing faintly as the curse began to hum through the air. Ty peeked out the window, his breath fogging the glass. "Uh, guys? He's not leaving."

Jason stood outside, his mask gleaming, his machete tapping steadily against the door. Every knock sent a shiver down El's spine, as if death itself was waiting patiently on the other side.

Becca pulled a crumpled piece of paper from her jacket pocket, her hands shaking as she smoothed it out on the projector's control panel. "This is the ritual. My dad left notes... but it's in pieces. We have to say it aloud, or the curse won't bind." El glanced at the symbols on the paper, his heart sinking. "This is gibberish. It's not even in English."

"It doesn't have to be perfect," Becca whispered, her voice cracking. "Just close enough."

The projector's hum grew louder, the symbols glowing brighter as the reel spun faster. The air inside the booth thickened, pressing against them like the walls were closing in. Cassie's voice was tight with panic. "Uh, *guys?*"

Jason's machete slammed against the glass, sending cracks spidering across the window. The door shuddered under his weight, the handle rattling violently. "We need to start the ritual!" Becca shouted.

El grabbed the paper and began reading, stumbling over the strange, guttural words. The symbols on the reel pulsed in time with his voice, filling the room with an eerie, glowing light.

As El read, the curse began to unfold—images flickering across the walls, scenes from movies merging and bleeding into each other. Zombies shambled through the fog, gremlins cackled in the distance, and Jason stood at the door, waiting to be unleashed.

The room vibrated with energy, the projector lens glowing white-hot. Becca joined in, her voice trembling but determined, and Cassie added her voice to the chant. The air buzzed with power, the words taking on a life of their own.

Outside, Jason's machete struck the glass again, shattering it completely. Rain poured into the booth, and the hulking figure stepped through the broken window, his shadow looming over them. El didn't stop reading. The ritual was their only chance, and they were running out of time. Becca's voice rose in pitch, matching the hum of the projector, and the cursed symbols glowed brighter, burning into the film reel.

Jason raised his machete, ready to strike— And then the projector *exploded* in a burst of light, throwing them all to the ground.

For a moment, everything was silent. The storm outside stilled, the monsters vanished, and the drive-in was plunged into darkness. El coughed, the acrid smell of burnt film filling his lungs. "Did it... did it work?" Cassie groaned, sitting up and brushing glass shards from her jacket. "I think... I think we did it."

Ty peeked out the broken window. "Jason's gone." Becca slumped against the wall, her hands shaking with relief. "We did it," she whispered, her voice thick with exhaustion. El exhaled, his heart still racing. "We actually did it." But just as they began to relax, a familiar sound echoed through the night—the soft, mechanical click of a projector starting up.

El's stomach dropped. "No... no, no, no..." They turned toward the broken projector, and to their horror, the reel began to spin again—this time on its own.

The film flickered to life, casting a new shadow on the wall. It wasn't Jason. It wasn't Michael.

It was something else entirely.

And the nightmare wasn't over yet.

Chapter 7: Battle in the Booth

October 14th, 1986 – Rustwood Drive-In, Projection Booth

The glow from the cursed reel spread through the booth like wildfire. Shadows stretched unnaturally across the walls, twisting into grotesque shapes that defied logic. The projector whirred, spinning faster and faster, as if it were possessed by the films it had played, sucking them back into life.

El's pulse raced as a new shape began to take form on the flickering screen—a figure unlike the slashers and creatures they had faced before. A low rumble vibrated through the room, followed by the chilling, distorted chant from *The Evil Dead*.

Cassie's breath hitched. "Oh no. Not *that* one." A clawed hand burst from the shadows, ripping through the screen on the booth's far wall. It was pale, writhing with veins that pulsed like worms under the skin. The hand gripped the edge of the screen, and slowly, grotesquely, a *deadite* began to crawl out, its teeth gnashing and blackened eyes rolling wildly in its head. El stumbled backward. "We need to finish the ritual! Now!"

"*No way!*" Ty gasped, fumbling with his jacket zipper. "That's a freakin' *deadite*! We're dead!" The deadite cackled, its laughter bouncing off the walls of the booth like nails scraping glass. Its grotesque, skeletal form slithered into the room, a creature pulled from the depths of pure nightmare.

Cassie grabbed a heavy film reel from the floor and braced herself. "Okay. We've survived Jason and Myers. What's one more?" Becca twisted the projector's controls, her hands flying over knobs and switches as she struggled to get the film to rewind. "It's not responding! The curse... it's overriding everything!"

El looked at the glowing reel and knew in his gut that the projector was no longer just a machine. It had become a gateway; an open door to every monster, every nightmare, that had ever lived on film. If they didn't close it, it wouldn't just consume them, it would consume *everything*.

The deadite lunged at Cassie, its jagged teeth snapping inches from her face. She swung the reel hard, cracking it across the deadite's skull with a metallic *clang*. "Not today, freakshow!" she growled, kicking it back toward the wall.

The deadite scrambled back up, its limbs twisting in impossible angles. A second hand burst from the wall behind it, pulling another writhing figure into the room. El's heart sank. They were multiplying.

"We need to stop this now!" Becca shouted, frantically flipping through her dad's notes. The storm outside raged harder, the wind howling through the shattered windows, scattering papers and debris across the booth.

El grabbed the reel and slammed it into the projector. "Just tell me what to say!" Becca's eyes scanned the notes, and she shouted over the wind, "We need to call the film back—bind it! Say this: *'By the light of the reel, by the seal of the lens, return to the screen and stay within!'*"

El, Cassie, and Ty shouted the words in unison:

"By the light of the reel, by the seal of the lens, return to the screen and stay within!"

The projector groaned, sputtering as the reel spun violently, casting sparks from its metal teeth. The deadites screeched as the light from the projector beam burned across their bodies, dragging them back toward the flickering screen. Their claws scraped desperately at the walls, but the pull of the reel was stronger.

Ty grabbed a broom handle and jabbed it at one of the creatures, pushing it toward the screen. "Back where you belong, ugly!" Cassie grinned through gritted teeth. "Look at us! We're basically Ghostbusters now!"

One by one, the deadites were sucked back into the screen, their distorted faces twisting as they vanished into the swirling void. The projector burned hotter, the lens glowing with an unnatural white light. The cursed reel whirled faster, threatening to overheat. "Almost there!" Becca yelled. "Keep going!"

Another figure clawed its way into the booth—this one larger, more grotesque, its skin sloughing off in chunks. It roared, a sound that reverberated through the room and sent shivers down El's spine.

"*Hurry!*" Ty shouted, holding the door shut as the storm outside threatened to blow it open. El's voice cracked as he shouted the binding words one last time. "*By the light of the reel, by the seal of the lens, return to the screen and stay within!*"

The projector exploded in a burst of blinding light, sending them all sprawling across the floor. Sparks rained down like confetti, and the cursed reel snapped from its frame, clattering to the ground with a metallic thud.

Silence fell over the room. The storm outside eased, the wind dying down to a low whisper. The flickering neon lights outside steadied, casting soft, eerie hues across the parking lot.

El sat up, coughing through the haze of smoke and burnt film. "Is it... is it over?" Becca stared at the projector, her hands trembling. The machine sat silent, the reel lying lifeless on the floor. "I think we did it." Ty let out a shaky laugh, slumping against the wall. "We're alive. We're actually alive."

Cassie grinned, brushing glass shards from her jacket. "Told you we could handle it." But as El helped Becca to her feet, a chilling thought gnawed at the back of his mind. Something still didn't feel right.

They all walked out into the night, reel in hand, a sense of unease still gripped them tight. Halfway across the lot they heard a low hum began. El dropped the reel in horror, and his heart sank. The cursed reel was cracked—only slightly, but enough to leave a jagged line across its surface. A faint hum lingered in the air, like the last breath of a dying machine. Cassie followed his gaze, her grin fading. "What now?" Becca swallowed hard, her voice barely audible. "If the reel's damaged... the curse isn't fully contained." The words hit them like a punch to the gut. "So... what does that mean?" Ty asked, dread creeping into his voice. Becca's eyes were wide with fear. "It means... this isn't over."

El's pulse quickened as he realized the truth: the monsters had been pulled back into the reel, but the door between film and reality was still cracked open. And if they didn't seal it soon, the nightmare would start all over again.

With the reel in hand, they braced themselves against the storm—ready to finish what they started.

The final act was just beginning.

Chapter 8: Ash vs. Reality

October 14th, 1986 – Rustwood Drive-In, Projection Booth and Lot

The storm outside surged with renewed fury, as if the night knew its grip was slipping. Lightning splintered the sky, illuminating the flooded parking lot in bursts of white and purple light. Rain hammered against the shattered windows of the projection booth, and somewhere in the distance, the faint hum of the projector sputtered back to life—one last gasp from the cursed machine.

El held the cracked reel like it was a ticking bomb. The jagged fracture in its metal glimmered under the dim glow of the booth's emergency lights. Cassie paced beside him, clenching and unclenching her fists. "What's the plan, El? We toss that reel into the nearest dumpster and hope the monsters don't crawl back out?"

Ty wiped the rain from his face with his sleeve. "What if we just *smash* it? End it right here?" Becca shook her head, panic simmering beneath her voice. "No. If the ritual isn't done properly, the curse could spread. Destroying the reel without sealing it could open a doorway even wider. This whole thing could spill out into the *real world*. Every monster, every horror—set free."

El's heart sank. There was no easy way out. "Then we finish what we started." Cassie sighed. "Of course we do. No movie ever ends without a dramatic final showdown, right?" She shot El a grin, but he could see the flicker of fear behind her bravado.

"We have to bind the reel, place it in the projector, and use it to pull everything back inside—every monster, every curse." Becca exclaimed. "How do we know it'll work?" Ty asked, his eyes darting toward the rain-streaked lot where shadows slithered between cars. "We don't," Becca whispered. "But if we don't try..." She trailed off, letting the unspoken horror hang in the air. Cassie tightened her grip on the broken broom handle she'd snagged earlier. "We finish this now.. No distractions."

"Yeah, because this night's been completely distraction-free so far," Ty muttered, rolling his eyes. El took a deep breath and placed the reel in the projector. The familiar, distorted voice of *The Evil Dead* filled the air again, followed by the ominous rattle of chains and the low growl of a chainsaw.

"Uh-oh," Cassie whispered, her eyes wide. "We've got company." A door on the far side of the lot flew open with a metallic clang, and there he was—Ash Williams, pulled straight from the *Evil Dead* films. His shirt was ripped, his face spattered with blood, and his trademark chainsaw roared to life in his right hand. The shotgun slung over his shoulder gleamed in the storm's light.

"Groovy," Ash muttered, giving them a grin that was equal parts heroic and insane. El stared in disbelief. "This... this can't be happening."

"Is that... *Ash?*" Ty stammered. "Like, *the* Ash?" Ash revved his chainsaw, his grin widening. "Looks like you kids are in some deep shit."

Cassie blinked, stunned. "Okay. I take back everything I said. This might actually be awesome." The deadites surged from the shadows, their twisted, skeletal forms shrieking as they closed in on the group. Ash's shotgun barked, and one of the creatures exploded into a cloud of black ichor.

El barely had time to process what was happening before Ash turned to them, raising his chainsaw. "You coming, or what? We've got monsters to kill."

The group sprinted toward the projector, Ash leading the charge with gleeful abandon. Chainsaw roaring, he hacked through the deadites like a man on a mission. El, Cassie, Ty, and Becca followed close behind, adrenaline pumping through their veins.

The storm raged harder, the projector flickering wildly as more figures crawled from the screen—each one more grotesque and terrifying than the last. Zombies shambled through the lot, slasher villains stalked in the shadows, and the gremlins cackled from the rooftops.

"Becca!" El shouted over the roar of the storm. "What do we do?" Becca yanked the cracked reel from her backpack and handed it to El. "Get it into the projector! I'll say the spell!"

El ran toward the booth, dodging a snarling gremlin that leapt from the hood of a car. He slammed the reel into the projector, his hands shaking as the cursed film began to unwind. "Now!" Becca shouted, her voice rising over the chaos.

The spell poured from her lips, the ancient words filling the night with a strange, otherworldly hum. The monsters screamed in protest as the projector's lens glowed brighter, pulling them back toward the screen.

Ash stood at the entrance, chainsaw revving, as he held the line against the horde. "Come on, you primitive screwheads!" he bellowed. "You're going *back* where you belong!"

The light from the projector intensified, dragging every nightmare creature into its beam. The deadites fought against the pull, their grotesque forms writhing in agony. Slashers stumbled, their masks slipping away like paper. One by one, the monsters were sucked back into the screen, their screams fading into the hum of the projector.

El held his breath, waiting for the reel to run its course. The air shimmered with energy, the line between film and reality blurring and folding in on itself. And then, with a final flash of light, the projector sputtered to a halt.

The monsters were gone. The night was still. El collapsed onto the ground, gasping for breath. Cassie dropped beside him, her grin wide and triumphant. "We did it," she whispered, her voice shaky with relief. "We actually did it."

Ty leaned against the booth, clutching his side. "I can't believe I'm saying this, but... that was kind of awesome." Ash slung his shotgun over his shoulder and gave them a wink. "Not bad, kids. Not bad at all."

Becca wiped the rain from her glasses, her eyes wide with disbelief. "Is... is it over?" El stared at the cracked reel in his hands, the faint hum of the projector still echoing in his ears.

"Yeah," he whispered. "It's over." Or so he hoped. Because in the world of horror, the credits never truly roll. Not for long.

Chapter 9: The Final Reel

October 14th, 1986 – Rustwood Drive-In, Projection Booth and Lot

The storm quieted, but the eerie hum of the cursed reel lingered, vibrating just beneath the surface of the night. El's heart still pounded in his chest, adrenaline mixing with exhaustion. The projector sat silent, the cracked reel inside glowing faintly, as if daring them to believe the nightmare was over.

"Tell me that's it," Ty muttered, catching his breath. "Tell me we're done." El glanced at the flickering screen outside, scanning the lot for movement. Rain dripped steadily from the hoods of the abandoned cars, but there were no zombies, no slashers, no deadites. Just silence.

"It feels too quiet," Becca whispered, clutching her Polaroid camera like it was a lucky charm. "Like... something's waiting." Ash stood near the door, shotgun still in hand, his eyes narrowed. "Kid's got a point. Evil never just rolls over."

Cassie exhaled slowly, tapping the side of the projector with a metallic *thunk*. "If this thing kicks back to life again, I'm burning the whole drive-in down." El turned to Becca. "How do we *really* finish this? No half measures—no mistakes."

Becca's eyes darkened as she studied the cracked reel. "We have to destroy it. Not just the reel—the whole thing. We seal the reel inside the projector and make sure it can never be played again. Ever."

"And how do we do that?" Ty asked warily. Cassie smirked. "I say we blow it to hell." Ash grinned. "Finally, someone with the right idea."

The plan formed quickly: they needed to bind the curse one final time, lock the reel inside the projector with the ritual's last incantation, and then destroy the whole thing. Becca explained it needed to be more than just smashing the projector—they'd have to perform the ritual exactly right. Only then could they ensure the projector wouldn't summon the monsters back—or worse, let something else crawl through.

Becca nodded. "If we do it right, the projector becomes a trap, sealing everything inside the reel for good." Ty looked around nervously. "And if we screw up?" Ash revved his chainsaw. "We don't screw up."

The four of them exchanged looks, a shared understanding that this was their last chance. Whatever happened, they had to see it through..

"Everyone, focus," Becca whispered. "This has to be perfect." They gathered around the projector, their voices blending as they repeated the final words of the ritual Becca had pieced together:

"By the light of the reel, by the seal of the lens, return to the screen and stay within!"

The projector groaned to life, the reel spinning slowly. For a moment, the lens cast distorted shadows onto the wall—brief flashes of monsters, flickering memories of every nightmare the cursed reel had summoned into existence. The images twisted and blurred, drawn back into the film like moths to a flame.

El felt a chill crawl up his spine as Michael Myers' mask flickered across the screen, followed by Jason's hulking form, snarling gremlins, and deadites clawing at the void. One by one, the horrors were sucked back into the reel, sealed inside by the rituals spell.

The reel spun faster, the hum growing louder as the projector fought against the ritual's final command. Sparks flew from the machine, and the lens glowed white-hot, as if the projector knew this would be its end. Cassie glanced at Ash, grinning. "Now or never."

Ash gave her a nod. "Groovy."

El grabbed the nearest can of lighter fluid from the booth's shelf, sloshing it over the projector. Cassie handed him a pack of matches, her eyes gleaming with determination. "Light it up."

With trembling hands, El struck a match. The tiny flame danced in the storm's wind, casting long shadows across their faces. He locked eyes with Becca, who gave him a firm nod. El tossed the match.

The fire roared to life, engulfing the projector in bright orange flames. The cursed reel hissed and popped, the symbols burning away as the magic unraveled. Smoke billowed out of the booth, thick and black, and the projector whined like a dying beast.

Cassie whooped, stepping back as the flames consumed everything. "Burn, baby, burn!"

The projector let out one final screech, a horrible, mechanical death rattle, and then the reel snapped, the symbols vanishing in a burst of light. The cursed film crumbled into ash, leaving behind only embers. For a long moment, none of them moved, waiting for something—*anything*—to crawl back from the flames. But the night remained still. The monsters were gone.

Ash slung his shotgun over his shoulder, a satisfied grin on his face. "Well, kids. Looks like you saved the day." Cassie gave him a playful salute. "Right back at you, hero."

Ty collapsed onto the ground, laughing breathlessly. "I can't believe we actually made it. I thought for sure we were toast." El wiped sweat from his brow, his legs trembling beneath him. "It's over. For real this time." Becca knelt beside the charred remains of the reel, poking at the ashes with a stick. "We did it... We really did it."

The storm outside began to ease, the clouds thinning as the first light of dawn crept over the horizon. The drive-in lot, once filled with nightmares, was now eerily quiet—just rows of empty cars, the flicker of neon signs, and the distant hum of an old radio struggling to find a signal.

As they stepped out of the booth and into the cool morning air, El felt a strange sense of peace settle over him. The horrors were over, the curse broken. But deep down, he knew this night would haunt them forever. Cassie nudged his shoulder, offering him a tired grin. "You did good, El."

He smiled back, his heart lighter than it had been all night. "We all did." Ash gave them one last nod, his chainsaw idling quietly. "It's been fun, kids. But I've got more deadites to hunt. Remember; shop smart, shop S-Mart" He winked, tipped an invisible hat, and sauntered off into the shadows, disappearing into the morning mist.

Becca leaned against El's shoulder, her voice soft. "Do you think this is really the end?" El stared at the smoldering remains of the projector. "Yeah," he whispered. "I think so."

Cassie arched an eyebrow. "Until the sequel, right?" El chuckled, the sound surprising even himself. "Yeah. Until the sequel."

The four of them stood there, side by side, as the first rays of sunlight bathed the ruined drive-in in gold. The nightmare was over, and the world—at least for now—was safe.

Epilogue: A New Beginning

September 12th, 1989 – Rustwood Drive-In, Forgotten and Buried in Time

The sun sagged low on the horizon, painting the sky in streaks of blood-red and bruised purple, like the dying embers of a fire no one remembered starting. The drive-in lay in ruins—an ancient skeleton of its former self, half-swallowed by creeping weeds and sunbaked asphalt cracked from years of neglect. Broken speakers dangled like nooses from weathered poles, their cords frayed and tangled. The screen—once a monolith of light and dreams—now stood warped and torn, an eerie grin of peeling paint stretched across its surface.

The place was a graveyard of memories, the ghosts of late-night showings and tailgate parties lingering in the air like stale popcorn grease and cigarette smoke. The wind whispered through rusted-out cars long since abandoned, stirring old ticket stubs buried beneath layers of dust. Time had tried its best to forget this place, but something lingered—an unseen spark waiting to reignite.

And then, from the far edge of the horizon, a lone car appeared. A 1977 Chevrolet Impala, its paint a faded seafoam green, tires kicking up a plume of dust that curled behind it like the tail of a dragon. It roared down the cracked highway, growing larger as it barreled toward the forgotten drive-in, leaving nothing but swirling dust in its wake. The engine coughed and sputtered as it approached the entrance gate—a gate hanging crooked on rusted hinges, barely holding on to a past no one remembered.

The car slid to a halt just inside the lot, the tires grinding against the gravel with a slow, deliberate groan. For a moment, everything stood still. The dust, kicked up from the long-forgotten road, whirled and spun around the car like a living thing, wrapping it in a cloud of swirling ash and dirt. The old drive-in, frozen in time, seemed to hold its breath.

Out of the swirling haze, the driver's door creaked open with a sharp metallic screech. A man stepped out, dust clinging to the sleeves of his denim jacket and the brim of his worn-out baseball cap. His boots crunched against the gravel as he took a step forward, scanning the ruins of the drive-in with slow, deliberate eyes. The sun, sinking deeper into the horizon, cast long shadows that stretched like claws over the lot.

The passenger door opened next, and out climbed a boy, no older than ten, with wide, curious eyes. He wore a T-shirt two sizes too big, featuring a faded logo for *The Goonies*. His sneakers scuffed against the ground as he stood next to the car, shielding his eyes against the settling dust with the back of his hand.

The man walked around the front of the Impala, his boots scraping the asphalt, until he stood beside the boy. He placed a reassuring arm over the kid's shoulder, squeezing it with a mix of pride and excitement, the kind of excitement that comes only from seeing the bones of something broken and knowing it can be made whole again.

"This is it, Mikey," the man said, his voice rough but warm, carrying the weight of promises yet to be fulfilled. "This is the place."

The boy stared at the ruined screen and the tangled mess of weeds sprouting through the cracked pavement. His small face lit up—not with the disappointment most kids would feel when staring at a forgotten relic, but with something closer to wonder. It was the look of someone who saw not what was, but what *could be*.

The man grinned, his expression full of possibility, as if he could already hear the hum of the projector firing back to life, smell the popcorn popping, and see the headlights bouncing off freshly painted poles. "We'll turn this into the best damn drive-in this town's ever seen," he said, his voice brimming with conviction. "A real double feature every Saturday night."

The boy's smile widened, his excitement bubbling over. "What movies?" he asked, the sparkle in his eyes matching the gleam of the dusty horizon.

The man grinned, his gaze sweeping over the broken speakers and the sagging screen, as if envisioning the future already written in the cracked asphalt and rusted poles. "Hellraiser," he said slowly, savoring the name. "And *Child's Play*." The boy's eyes widened with delight. "That's gonna be *so cool!*"

"Yeah," the man said, pulling his son closer. "Yeah, it is."

Together, they stood there, father and son, surveying the ruins of the Rustwood Drive-In with the kind of wonder and hope only dreamers can muster. They didn't see the weeds or the broken screen—they saw the crowds, the lights, the magic waiting to come alive again.

And as the last light of the sun dipped below the horizon, the old projector—hidden deep within the booth—hummed softly to itself, a faint, almost imperceptible sound, like the memory of a reel spinning long ago.

In the quiet dusk, dust and time settled around them, and the wind carried a single word whispered across the empty lot:

"Action."

Be on the look out for the next books in
The Retro Horrors: The Lost Decades series'

Endless Paths: The Choose-Your-Doom Chronicles

"Every choice opens a new path. But some paths are dead ends... literally."

When Jordan H. and his friends find an old *Choose Your Own Adventure* book at a forgotten bookstore, it seems like a harmless throwback—until the game begins to bleed into their lives. With each turn of the page, reality shifts, and the book's sinister challenges come to life around them.

Lost in a world where every choice could be their last, the group must solve puzzles, navigate eerie landscapes, and survive the dark forces chasing them. The stakes grow higher as twisted reflections, shadowy figures, and a mysterious figure known only as the Gamekeeper emerge to test their courage—and their friendship.

But as the game's rules begin to unravel, Jordan discovers that the only way out may be to rewrite the ending. And not everyone will survive to see the final page.

In *Endless Paths*, the lines between fantasy and nightmare blur, and every decision has consequences. Will you choose the right path... or get lost in the maze forever?

"Not all books close when you're done reading."

The Forgotten Carnival

In the summer of 1987, a mysterious carnival appears overnight on the outskirts of a small town—its glowing lights and haunting music promising dreams fulfilled. But for Jake, Riley, Amber, Dare, and Jimmy, **the carnival offers only fear, twisted reflections of their worst nightmares, and a sinister game they never asked to play.** When Jimmy disappears inside the carnival, the friends must venture deeper into its surreal horrors to rescue him.

But nothing in this carnival is what it seems. **The rides don't just thrill—they consume. The fortune-teller knows too much, and the grinning ringmaster, Mr. Grin, grows stronger with every scream.** As the teens confront mirror versions of themselves and rides that steal years from their souls, they uncover the carnival's terrible secret: **It's alive, feeding on fear—and it never lets anyone leave.**

To escape, they must face their darkest fears and unravel the carnival's curse before it traps them forever. But even if they survive, **the carnival may not be finished with them yet.**

Filled with eerie nostalgia, 80s pop culture, and relentless tension, The Forgotten Carnival is a pulse-pounding horror adventure about friendship, fear, and the battle to hold onto hope when everything feels like a nightmare.

The Polaroid Project

In the summer of 1982, four high school friends stumble upon an old Polaroid camera at a dusty flea market tucked between cassette tapes and neon fanny packs. At first, it seems like a harmless relic—something to capture their skate park tricks and mixtape swaps. But the photos it prints reveal something terrifying: future moments they aren't prepared to witness. A shattered glass window. Blood on the pavement. A girl's face, pale and lifeless—someone they don't recognize but must find.

As the camera continues to spit out photographs that defy explanation, the friends realize the images are more than warnings. They're *prophecies*—glimpses of events that haven't happened yet but are destined to unless they can intervene. One picture shows a familiar graffiti-covered wall and a girl named Susie, who disappeared five years ago under mysterious circumstances.

Every shot, every clue, pulls them deeper into a haunting urban legend that whispers about an ancient curse connected to the town's abandoned roller rink. With the night of a lunar eclipse fast approaching, the group faces a terrifying truth: change the course of fate, or become the next victims captured on film.

Neon Dreams

A group of friends obsessed with Dungeons & Dragons finds themselves trapped in a dream world after a bizarre séance during a sleepover. The dreamscape mirrors the neon-lit streets of their town but is haunted by creatures from their campaigns. The kids must rely on their D&D skills and friendships to navigate the dangerous dream world, defeat an ancient evil called "The Architect," and wake up before their dreams consume them.

1980s Nostalgia: Glow-in-the-dark dice, D&D figurines, soda cans littering the table, VHS horror rentals, and a soundtrack filled with synthwave and power ballads.

Key Elements: Nightmarish dream sequences, a villain inspired by Lovecraftian horrors, strange overlaps between dreams and reality, and the idea that imagination can become both a weapon and a trap.

Also by B. Humphrey

Retro Horrors: The Lost Decade
Cassette Ghosts
Summer of the Black Star
The Arcade Incident
Dead End Drive – In

The Autumn Folklore Chronicles
The Forest Of Forgotten Names
The Witch Of Windspindle Hollow
The Burrowfolk Chronicles

The Phantom Finders Club
A Haunting On Maplewood Street
The Secrets Of Old Fort Tower
Ghosts OF The Infirmary

www.ingramcontent.com/pod-product-compliance
Lightning Source LLC
Chambersburg PA
CBHW061637130726
47996CB00003B/1328